Check out these other exciting
▼ STECK-VAUGHN Adventures!

Get ready for a bumpy ride! Travel on
SNAKE RIVER

Where there's smoke. . . there's fire
Read all about it in
SMOKE

Is there any truth to the old pirate's poem?
Find out in
FORGOTTEN TREASURE

They're burning rubber in the desert heat!
See who in
ROAD RALLY

Is the big prize worth a big risk?
Get the answer in
VIDEO QUEST

Danger lies where eagles soar. Find out why in
SOARING SUMMER

Knight makes right? See how in
KNIGHT MOVES

The chase is on — but who's hunting who?
Find out, read
DANGEROUS GAME

A family can survive anything, right?
Learn more in
SNOW TREK

ISBN 0-8114-9313-X

9 04

Produced by Mega-Books of New York, Inc.
Design and Art Direction by Michaelis/Carpelis Design Assoc.

Cover illustration: Matthew Archambault

DON'T LOOK BACK

by Himilce Novas

interior illustrations by
Larry Raymond

STECK-VAUGHN®
C O M P A N Y

CHAPTER 1

Rasheed Johnson couldn't believe his own eyes.

"Wow!" he cried to his buddy, Leonard Williams. "These mountains are awesome, man!"

"No kidding!" exclaimed Leonard. He adjusted his heavy knapsack.

The bus that had dropped the boys off at the Joseph Earl Jones Wilderness Camp disappeared around the sharp bend. Rasheed and Leonard were all alone, surrounded by mountains and forests.

"Joseph Earl Jones must be some kind of smart guy to have gotten himself a place like this," said Leonard.

The boys saw a small sign with an arrow pointing left. Rasheed and Leonard headed in that direction.

Their bus had left the city a little late, so the two boys walked quickly.

They figured Mr. Jones and the other people here for the three-day Wilderness Weekend were probably already at the camp.

The two boys spotted the camp office. Leonard caught sight of Mr. Jones, the tall, fit camp director. He stood in the office doorway waving to the boys.

"He sure is big!" Rasheed said. He started to walk a little faster.

Mr. Jones was a Vietnam vet. He looked like a tough guy, but Rasheed and Leonard had heard there wasn't anything mean or macho about him.

Rasheed made sure he was first to shake hands with Mr. Jones. It was just what Leonard expected of Rasheed.

The two boys had been best buddies since grade school, as close as real

brothers. But Rasheed had this thing about always being first. "Just keep going and don't look back," was Rasheed's motto. It was nothing the two boys ever talked about. But sometimes it really bothered Leonard.

"Welcome, boys!" Mr. Jones warmly

greeted them. "You must be Rasheed and Leonard! You're just in time for supper. Have a seat." Mr. Jones pointed to a picnic table nearby. When he spoke, he sounded like he was giving orders, just like an army officer.

Rasheed rushed to the table to meet the others. Leonard sat down next to him. They introduced themselves to Ralph and Juan, the other two boys. But Rasheed just nodded at the two girls, Tiffany and Maggie. Leonard shook their hands.

Everyone relaxed and chatted. Mr. Jones served up plates of fried trout and wild mushrooms.

"Everything Mr. Jones cooks, he catches or picks himself," said Tiffany. She looked at Rasheed and Leonard with a big, friendly smile.

The six teenagers ate with gusto. The mountain air had made them hungry.

"Well, kids, let's get to work!" Mr. Jones said when all their plates were empty.

"We're going trekking right away?" asked Rasheed.

Leonard was excited at the thought of going out in the woods at night. He stood up, ready for adventure.

"Not so fast!" said Mr. Jones, smiling. "The first kind of work we learn in this camp is called cooperation. You can't survive in the woods without it!"

"What kind of cooperation are you talking about, Oh-great-wilderness-master?" joked Leonard.

Leonard could be a real cut-up, especially when he was happy.

"I mean doing things like helping with the dishes for starters," said Mr. Jones. The camp director handed Leonard a pile of greasy plates. Then he pointed toward the kitchen inside the main log cabin.

The four boys and two girls trooped in to attack the dirty dishes. They were done in ten minutes flat. Then everybody regrouped at the picnic table.

"I want to run through our plans for

the next three days," Mr. Jones told the group. "Our big wilderness trek to the top of Mount Aspen will be on Sunday. To get ready for that, you'll need to learn a few things first."

"What kinds of skills will we be working on?" asked Rasheed.

"Tomorrow we'll focus on working together in what we call 'tight teams,' " answered Mr. Jones. "Then you will learn basic wilderness skills, like how to catch fish!"

"And how to set up a tent, how to start a campfire, and how to cook those fish." A woman's voice finished Mr. Jones's speech.

Rasheed and Leonard turned around. A friendly looking woman had stepped up behind them. She was dressed in jeans and an all-weather jacket.

"Mcet my partner, kids! This is Ms. Patricia Velez Miranda," smiled Mr. Jones. "You'll be working very closely with her for the next three days."

Leonard and Rasheed looked at each other. Rasheed shook his head.

"I can't believe a woman's going to teach us how to survive in the woods!" Rasheed whispered to his friend.

"Don't worry," Leonard whispered back. "I'll bet you she knows what she's doing."

"I'll bet she doesn't. But that's okay. I don't plan on listening to her anyway," said Rasheed.

CHAPTER 2

The next morning Rasheed and Leonard woke up at the same time. Their tiny log cabin felt like a warm cocoon. There were no fire engine sirens blasting outside the window. There were no trucks honking away. There were only birds chirping and leaves rustling.

"We're definitely not in the city anymore," yawned Rasheed.

"Don't you miss those early morning car alarms?" joked Leonard.

"Up and at 'em!" Mr. Jones cried from outside the cabin window.

"Rise and shine!" added Ms. Miranda. "Everybody wash and dress!

Breakfast is waiting for you on the picnic table. We'll see you on Hill Number Three in forty-five minutes sharp!"

"Forty-five minutes!" Leonard growled. He watched his roommate make a beeline for the bathroom.

"Sure!" Rasheed said, sticking his head under the faucet. "I'll bet we can make it in thirty—at least I can!"

Forty-five minutes later, a sleepy group stumbled up the hill. They had found it by reading a big sign marked "Number 3." The hill was low, wide, and flat on top.

"This will be our base camp," explained Ms. Miranda.

"Do you all know what a base camp is?" asked Mr. Jones.

"A place where you start from and come back to," piped up Rasheed before anyone else could answer.

"Very good!" nodded Mr. Jones. "Base camp is a place you're all going to get to

love after spending a few hours hiking up in the mountains!"

"So let's get started," said Ms. Miranda. "Now, let's see: Leonard and Rasheed, step out here in front. Tiffany and Juan, come over here. And Maggie and Ralph, step over here."

"These are the tight teams I talked about yesterday," said Mr. Jones.

"We're sure to be the best," whispered Rasheed to Leonard. "Juan and Ralph don't stand a chance with girls as their teammates!"

Ms. Miranda gave the instructions. Each tight team had to find its cave hidden somewhere in the bushes about half a mile from base camp. There were three caves altogether. When they found their cave, each team had to stick their flag at the entrance. They also had to write down what time they arrived. Then they were to return to base camp.

Ms. Miranda handed each team a detailed map and a different-colored flag. Rasheed and Leonard got the red one.

"Okay, head out!" she said. "We'll be waiting for you here."

Rasheed and Leonard had never seen a map like this before. There were different trails marked on it. There were labels for streams, hills, and forests. There was a compass rose on the right side of the map. It showed north, south, east, and west. Leonard and Rasheed's

cave was marked on the map with their initials and a drawing of a red flag.

"It's like a pirate's treasure map!" said Rasheed.

"No, it isn't," said Leonard. "It's an explorer's map!"

"Okay, whatever you say," said Rasheed. "Let's go find our cave!"

"This way!" said Leonard. He pointed to some trees on the left and held up the map for Rasheed to see.

"I think it's to the right," said Rasheed, glancing at the map. "Just follow me and don't look back!"

"All right, Rasheed," said Leonard. "You go right and I'll go left. We'll see who finds the cave first!"

"But we can't, Leonard," Rasheed argued. "We have to find it together! We're a tight team! Remember what Mr. Jones said about cooperation?"

"Of course! So why don't you just start cooperating with me?" snapped Leonard. "The most direct route is to

the left, down this path. See? It goes
along this cliff marked on the map."

"Don't be ridiculous, Leonard! It'll
take forever to climb up the cliff," said
Rasheed. "It's better to take this path to
the right. Even if it's a little longer."

"That's what you think, Rasheed! I
can read this map a lot better than you!"
argued Leonard. "I'm going to the left!"
He stormed down the path.

"I'll bet I'll beat you to the cave!" Rasheed shouted after Leonard. He took the other path.

An hour and a half later, Leonard found Rasheed waiting outside their cave. Rasheed had his arms folded over his chest. He glared at Leonard.

"That cliff was higher and steeper than it looks on the map," muttered Leonard. "I couldn't climb it. I had to

turn back and follow your path."

The boys headed back towards the base following the path that Rasheed had taken. There they found Ms. Miranda waiting for them.

"Hey, what happened to you guys?" she asked. "I figured you'd be here at least twenty minutes ago!"

"We had to take a long detour around this cliff," said Leonard.

"But there's an easy way to get over that cliff. All you had to do was give Rasheed a leg up. Then he could have reached down and given you a hand up," said Ms. Miranda. "Didn't you think of that?"

The boys gave sheepish looks.

Leonard felt bad. It seemed like he and his buddy had somehow messed up from the get-go.

"Did the other kids find their caves all right?" asked Leonard.

"Everyone else did really well," answered Ms. Miranda. "I kept looking for you guys, but you were nowhere in sight!"

She didn't look too pleased.

"Oh, man!" Rasheed said under his breath. "Does that mean we lost to the girls? We can't let them do better than we do!"

CHAPTER 3

After lunch, Leonard decided to wander down to the trout stream and do some fishing on his own. He had found a great fishing pole back in the cabin.

As Leonard approached the stream, he was surprised to find Tiffany standing knee-deep in the water. In her hands was a fishing rod. With one easy motion, she cast her fishing line into the stream.

"Hi, Leonard!" Tiffany called when she caught sight of him.

"I didn't know you could fish, Tiffany," said Leonard.

"My grandmother taught me when I

was little. She loves the outdoors," answered Tiffany. "If you want, I'll show you how to cast."

"That would be great," smiled Leonard.

Tiffany waded back to the bank of the stream. "First of all, this is a special kind of hook called a fly," she said. "It's made to look like an insect because trout love bugs."

"So that's why they call it fly fishing," smiled Leonard.

"Exactly," answered Tiffany. "Now, the trick is to cast the line gently. Then you flick your wrist so the fly moves like a bug in the water."

"Hi, guys!"

Leonard saw Rasheed waving and coming towards them. Then, all at once, he saw Maggie, Juan, and Ralph walking towards the stream, too.

"Oh, no," Leonard muttered to himself. "Just when Tiffany and I were getting to know each other, here comes

the whole gang!"

"What did you say, Leonard?" asked Tiffany. She cast her line gently into the stream.

"Nothing. I guess we're having a regular powwow," answered Leonard.

Rasheed and the rest of the group

gathered at the edge of the stream. Leonard quickly picked up his fishing pole and tried to cast the line into the water.

"Whoa, Leonard, since when do you know how to fish?" shouted Rasheed.

"Tiffany showed me how. Watch me now! It's all in the wrist!"

Just as Leonard spoke, he felt a tug on the fishing line.

"Hey, I think I caught something!" shouted Leonard. He tugged the line sharply.

"Well, reel it in!" cried Tiffany.

Everyone stopped talking. All eyes were on Leonard.

The tug on the fishing line was so strong that Leonard was sure he had caught a huge trout. He pulled hard on the fishing pole.

Suddenly, Leonard was flying backwards through the air. He landed on the seat of his pants. The whole group burst into laughter. The pole had snapped in two and there was no fish in sight!

"Hey, good job Leonard!" cried Rasheed.

"That's no way to catch a fish!" said a voice behind them. It was Mr. Jones.

"I think it's about time we started with those wilderness skills. We'll begin with fishing. Now everybody run to your cabins and get your poles!"

When the group returned with their

fishing poles, Mr. Jones had them gather around. "Watch carefully!" he said.

Mr. Jones waded into the stream and cast his line into deep water, away from the rocks.

"Never cast into the rocks, or else your line might get caught!"

Leonard looked embarrassed.

"Now you kids are responsible for dinner tonight. You'd better get started on the main course!" laughed Mr. Jones. He handed Leonard his own pole.

"What if we don't catch anything?" asked Leonard.

"Don't worry, Leonard," said Tiffany. "It's about cooperation, remember? Besides, who could eat a whole fish alone?" she winked.

"Okay, you guys," boasted Rasheed. "Just you watch. I'm going to catch the first fish!"

Everyone took his or her pole and waded into the water, headed in

different directions. Leonard worked
hard on casting the line and making the
fly "swim" like a bug. He had to catch a
trout before Rasheed. He just had to!

Juan and Ralph got a few nibbles, but
no bites. Maggie got some nibbles, too.
Tiffany nearly caught a trout, but it
came off her line as she reeled it in.

Rasheed cast into the deep water. He
had a nibble. Before he knew it, a huge
trout grabbed the fly on the end of his
line. He strained to reel the big fish in.
It seemed to take forever. Finally,

Rasheed pulled a large trout out of the water.

Everyone gathered around to admire the catch.

"Wow!" cried Rasheed. "That was great! Nothing can top that! This is big enough to feed everybody!"

"Cool, Rasheed, really cool," Leonard said. Then he muttered under his breath, "We'll see how long your luck holds out!"

CHAPTER 4

By three o'clock that afternoon, the group had caught seven trout.

"Okay, kids! Let's get all those trout into the buckets. Gather around so we can go over the next steps with Ms. Miranda," called Mr. Jones.

"These next skills are very important. They're going to save you when you're out in the woods!" said Ms. Miranda. "Is everyone with me?"

"Yeah!" the group cried.

"Okay," said Mr. Jones. "Then let's learn how to build a campfire."

Mr. Jones handed each tight team a bag of firewood and a box of waterproof matches.

"If you're ever going to camp outdoors, you need to build a good fire," said Mr. Jones. "That way you can keep warm and cook food!"

"Like those trout you just caught!" added Ms. Miranda. She pointed to the fish in the bucket.

"Is there anyone here who doesn't know how to build a fire?" asked Mr. Jones.

No one spoke up.

"Rasheed and Leonard," Ms. Miranda called, "you go first. Build a fire over here. Then the other teams will get to work."

"I read in some adventure books that you put the kindling, like dry leaves and sticks, on the bottom," Rasheed told Leonard. "Then you stack larger pieces of wood on top. You light it at the base."

"In this movie I saw, they put the kindling on top of the logs," answered Leonard.

"Leonard, you've got it all

backwards," argued Rasheed.

"Your way is wrong!" snarled Leonard.

"My way is right!" snapped Rasheed.

"Do you always have to be a know-it-all, Rasheed?" cried Leonard. He quickly piled the kindling on top of a pile of logs.

"Okay, I've done my best," sighed

Rasheed. "Go ahead and fall on your face again if that's what you want to do!"

Leonard lit a match and ignited the kindling. It burned, but the larger pieces of wood didn't catch fire. Soon all the flames went out.

"What did I tell you, Leonard!" said Rasheed. "Now I have to search for more kindling to start this fire!"

A few minutes later, Rasheed had a fire burning nicely. It roared in a neat stack and gave off a lot of heat.

"That was just luck, Rasheed!" muttered Leonard. Leonard resented Rasheed for being the one to build the fire—just like he resented Rasheed for showing off at the trout stream.

Ms. Miranda walked over and admired Rasheed's handiwork. "Did you guys work together on this one?" she asked.

"Sort of," answered Leonard.

Ms. Miranda looked unhappy.

"Well, let's move on to the next wilderness skill," she said. Ms. Miranda gave each team a tent. "Watch how I put this tent together."

"We already know how to do that," chimed Leonard and Rasheed.

The boys quickly put together their tent.

"That was easy!" said Leonard with a big smile.

Ms. Miranda came over to check their work. She stared at the tent.

"Guys," she said, frowning, "can't you

work together? There's a big problem here. If a strong wind blows, your tent will end up on the other end of the country!"

Leonard realized that Rasheed had not done his part of the job, fastening the tent to the ground with stakes. He grabbed a few stakes. One by one, he pounded them into the ground.

"Much better. Good job, Leonard!" said Ms. Miranda.

Leonard smiled. He felt that he was finally beginning to show Rasheed a thing or two.

After setting up the tents, the group gathered around Mr. Jones.

"You kids did really well. Now let's do some exercises to prepare for the wilderness trek tomorrow," said Mr. Jones.

Everyone did stretches and a set of sit-ups and push-ups. After that, they ran a twelve-minute course along the trout stream. Well warmed up, the

group gathered around Ms. Miranda.

"See that long knotted rope hanging from that big tree over there?" asked Ms. Miranda. "I want both members of each team to scale the rope as quickly as possible. Watch."

In a flash, Ms. Miranda grabbed the end of the rope. She pulled with her hands and pushed with her legs, crossed at the ankles. She shimmied to the top with amazing ease. Then she quickly slid back down.

"Let's make speed count, kids!" shouted Mr. Jones. "Let's see which team is the fastest!"

Juan and Tiffany were the first to get started. The rest of the group watched. Juan reached the top quickly. Tiffany was almost as fast as Ms. Miranda.

Then Ralph and Maggie went. Ralph got off to a slow start, but he made up for it by coming back down in a flash. He and Maggie beat Juan and Tiffany's time by only three seconds.

"Great!" said Mr. Jones, looking at his stopwatch. "Now it's Rasheed and Leonard's turn. Go for it, guys!"

"Come on, Leonard! Don't look back!" said Rasheed. The boys made a dash for the rope.

Leonard grabbed the rope and quickly climbed to the top. After he climbed back down, he handed the rope to Rasheed.

Rasheed took the rope firmly in his hand. Then he paused for a moment. He seemed unsure of himself.

"Let's go, Rasheed!" cried Leonard.

Rasheed started to crawl up the rope. He made it to the top. But when he had climbed halfway down, he looked at the ground below him. Suddenly, he froze.

"Hey, Rasheed! What's the matter with you?" Leonard shouted from below.

"I got a rope splinter in my hand!" cried Rasheed.

"Oh, man! Keep going! Get down here!" said Leonard. "How could you stop for a lousy splinter, Rasheed!"

In a few seconds, Rasheed finally reached the ground. Even though Leonard had been the fastest one in the whole group, he and Rasheed came in last.

"Let Mr. Jones check that splinter, Rasheed," frowned Ms. Miranda.

"Oh, it's okay. I got it out myself," answered Rasheed.

Mr. Jones threw his arm around both

of the boys' shoulders.

"Nice try, my friends," he said in a warm voice. "But you're going to have to learn a little more about cooperation. Folks have to help each other, even encourage each other. You know what I mean?"

"Sort of," answered Leonard.

"Sleep on it tonight," Ms. Miranda added. "You've got to be ready for the really tough stuff tomorrow." She turned and walked away.

CHAPTER 5

Rasheed and Leonard couldn't believe the day of the wilderness trek had finally arrived.

Ms. Miranda and Mr. Jones gave the whole group a big pep talk at breakfast that morning. Then, at base camp, they handed each tight team a map and a backpack with matches, a tent, water, and sandwiches.

Each tight team had to trek through the wilderness from a different starting point, find Mount Aspen, and get to the clearing at the top.

When a team arrived, they had to stick their flag in the ground. Then the team had to set up their tent and build a small fire. Mr. Jones and Ms. Miranda would be watching from a secret lookout. They would log in what time they saw each flag and each fire. The first team to finish all the tasks would win. The prize was two tickets to the biggest pro basketball game of the season!

"We've mapped out a route for each team," said Mr. Jones. "Each route is the same length and has the same degree of difficulty."

"Follow your route carefully, kids," warned Ms. Miranda.

"Sure thing!" Rasheed spoke up for the whole group.

Leonard sat on the ground, studying the map and their route.

"What are you waiting for, Leonard? Let's get going!" said Rasheed. He glanced down at the map. "We'll go down this trail here . . . then around this bend by the trout stream! Just start hiking and don't look back!"

"But I think we should study the map and get the whole lay of the land first. You know, like in the movies and stuff," said Leonard.

"That's fine for the movies, Leonard. But we have a race to win! Remember those basketball tickets!" answered Rasheed.

The two boys hiked for about half an hour. Every turn took them deeper into the forest.

After all the prep work, it was exciting for the boys to be finally on their own.

Rasheed and Leonard hiked beside the trout stream. Along the way, they saw rabbits, soaring hawks, and even a couple of deer. The stream headed into a small ravine.

"Hey, Leonard, do you think the other guys are trekking faster than we are?" asked Rasheed.

"There's no way of telling," answered Leonard. "But the map says we have to go past this ravine. After that, we go around a big bend. That should bring us in sight of Mount Aspen."

"Maybe we can find a shortcut!" said Rasheed.

"I don't see how," answered Leonard. He studied the map. "Ms. Miranda said to make sure to follow the map exactly. And there aren't any shortcuts on the map!"

They stopped near the edge of the small ravine and took a drink of water

from their canteens.

Rasheed looked down into the ravine. Suddenly he felt lightheaded.

"On second thought, Rasheed, you may be right," said Leonard. "This map says we have to go all the way around the bend to get to a bridge. The bridge takes us across to Mount Aspen."

"So, what are you getting at?" answered Rasheed.

"Well," said Leonard with a familiar twinkle in his eye. Rasheed knew that twinkle meant trouble. "What if we find a way across this ravine right here, instead of hiking all the way around the bend? That would put us right on Mount Aspen and within minutes of winning the prize!"

Rasheed gave Leonard a long, cold hard stare.

"And just how do you think we can do that? You think we can just jump across this ravine?" asked Rasheed.

"Nothing that crazy," said Leonard. "You see that tree trunk lying across the ravine?"

"What about it?" asked Rasheed.

"That can be our bridge!" exclaimed Leonard. "The ravine isn't too wide. The trunk looks sturdy, but not too thick. We can scale it, just like we did when we crawled up that rope."

Rasheed stared at the tree trunk lying across the ravine.

"We'd have our flag and tent on Mount Aspen," Leonard continued, "at least a half hour before anyone else got there!"

Rasheed continued to stare at the tree trunk. Then he looked down. It felt as though he were standing on top of a skyscraper. He was getting dizzy.

"I don't know," said Rasheed. "It looks

pretty dangerous. What if we slip?"

"We won't! It's a short crossing. It's just a few yards to the other side," said Leonard. "Just grab the trunk and swing out into space!"

"But it's more than a few yards down," Rasheed said, almost to himself.

"Come on," Leonard urged. "You know how to get across, right? Just watch out for splinters this time!"

Rasheed thought about it for a moment. It felt like too big a risk. But then again, he didn't want Leonard to think he was chicken. And he certainly didn't want to tell Leonard about his secret fear.

"Okay," Rasheed said finally. He had a queasy feeling in his stomach.

Leonard went first. He crawled to the edge of the ravine and grabbed the slim tree trunk easily. Then he quickly made his way across the trunk. When Leonard got to the other side, he swung his feet onto the other ledge and stood up.

Rasheed slid himself to the edge slowly. He squeezed his hands around the trunk. Then he began to follow his buddy. Rasheed kept his eyes straight in front of him. He moved slowly.

"Come on, man!" called out Leonard. He was already looking ahead for the trail. Suddenly, a piece of bark loosened from the trunk in front of Rasheed. He watched it fall to the bottom of the ravine. Rasheed froze.

It looked like a bottomless pit beneath his dangling feet. His heart was pounding like a drum. His shirt was damp with sweat.

"Keep going, man!" Leonard yelled from the other side.

Rasheed was frozen stiff, hanging on to the tree trunk.

"What's the matter, Rasheed?" shouted Leonard.

"I can't . . . I can't move, Leonard!" cried Rasheed in a faint, frightened voice.

"Why not?" Leonard screamed. He thought Rasheed was faking. He was angry that his buddy was making them lose precious time.

"I'm scared!" Rasheed said, "I don't think I'm going to make it!"

CHAPTER 6

Leonard didn't know what to do. He looked up at the top of Mount Aspen. He could just feel those hot basketball tickets in his hands.

There was no time to lose. For a moment, he felt like just leaving Rasheed behind to fend for himself. That would teach him for being such a big shot when he caught that trout and built that fire! It would serve Rasheed right, even if he really was stuck!

"Rasheed!" Leonard cried out. He cupped his hands to his mouth. "Are you kidding or something?"

"No, I'm not! I'm scared of heights! I never told anybody! I can't move,

Leonard, I really can't!"

"Don't be a fool, Rasheed! This is no time to be chicken!" shouted Leonard. "Just get yourself over here fast!"

"Hey, Leonard, let's talk a little cooperation here. Let's help your teammate, huh?" Ms. Miranda had appeared right at Leonard's side.

She grabbed onto the tree trunk. Then, Ms. Miranda made her way out to Rasheed. She was face to face with the frightened boy.

It suddenly dawned on Leonard that his buddy's life really was in danger. He remembered how Rasheed had stopped halfway down the rope the day before. Rasheed had said it was because of a rope splinter. But maybe it was because he was afraid. Was he really that scared of heights?

"Hey, Rasheed!" called Leonard in a strong voice, "We're going to get you over here! Don't worry. Did you hear me, man?"

"Uh huh," answered Rasheed faintly.

He was still hanging tightly to the tree trunk.

"Okay, look at me," said Ms. Miranda softly. Everything's going to be just fine!" Rasheed raised his eyes and looked into hers.

"Now I want you to follow me. Do what I do. We'll take it slowly," continued Ms. Miranda.

She looked straight at Rasheed as she began to back herself up. Ms. Miranda moved slowly, keeping close to the boy.

Leonard waited for Rasheed to make

a move. At first, Rasheed didn't budge. But Ms. Miranda kept repeating, "Everything's going to be okay. Keep looking at me. Just keep looking at me." Slowly, Rasheed inched forward.

"Great! Keep moving with me, Rasheed," said Ms. Miranda.

"Way to go!" echoed Leonard.

Leonard held his breath. He wasn't sure his buddy would make it. Rasheed looked really tired—and really scared. Leonard held his breath. Rasheed moved his hands forward.

"That's the way, champ!" shouted Leonard. "Yeah, you're doing it! Easy!"

Ms. Miranda made her way slowly across the trunk back to where Leonard was standing. Rasheed never took his eyes off her. He copied her every move.

"Just a few more moves, Rash! Yeah, a little more. One more. Yeah! You made it, man! You made it!" cried Leonard. Ms. Miranda swung onto the ground and pulled Rasheed up from the edge of the tree trunk.

When Rasheed finally stood on firm ground, Leonard hugged him and punched him playfully on the shoulder.

"That was a close call, boys," said Ms. Miranda.

"How did you know we were in trouble, Ms. Miranda?" Leonard asked.

"Mr. Jones and I were on our secret lookout watching the teams through our binoculars. I know every stick and stone

in this area. When I saw you guys stop near the ravine, I figured you might just try to cross this trunk!"

Suddenly, Leonard remembered the race. "Hey, let's get to the top, Rash! Maybe we still have time!" cried Leonard.

"Wait a minute, boys. You broke the rules," said Ms. Miranda sternly. "You were supposed to follow the map exactly. Instead you put each other's life in danger. For that, you've got to forfeit the race."

The boys bowed their heads.

"I guess the only thing we can do now is go back to base camp," said Rasheed sadly.

"I'm afraid so," nodded Ms. Miranda.

Rasheed and Leonard felt bad as they followed Ms. Miranda back to base camp. They had lost the race—and the tickets to the basketball game.

"That sure was tense at the ravine," said Leonard as they followed Ms.

Miranda along the trail.

"I should have told you sooner about my fear of heights," said Rasheed. "It's my fault."

"We're both to blame," answered Leonard.

"I guess one of those girls won," said Rasheed softly. "Maybe they do make good teammates after all."

"You might not even be alive if it

weren't for Ms. Miranda!" answered Leonard.

Ten minutes after the boys got back to base camp, the other two teams arrived. Tiffany and Juan were laughing and kidding each other. They had been the first to the clearing on Mount Aspen. And they were the first to set up a tent and build a fire.

"That was really fun!" Tiffany smiled to Leonard and Rasheed. "We waited a while for you guys, but you never showed up. What happened?"

The boys looked down at the ground in silence.

The group gathered around. Mr. Jones and Ms. Miranda presented Tiffany and Juan with the basketball tickets. Everybody congratulated them.

Then Mr. Jones and Ms. Miranda looked at Rasheed and Leonard. The two boys looked at each other. It was hard to speak up before the whole group.

"Well, come on, you guys. Tell us what happened!" piped up Tiffany.

Leonard nudged Rasheed. "Don't you always like to be first?" he joked nervously. Rasheed swallowed hard. Then he began.

"Well, I told Leonard we should find a shortcut and be the first team on Mount Aspen," said Rasheed. "But the shortcut turned into a nightmare!"

"Yeah," nodded Leonard. "Instead of following our route across a bridge, we crossed this ravine by crawling across a

tree trunk. I was fine. But Rasheed froze halfway across the trunk."

"Luckily, Ms. Miranda came along and saved me," added Rasheed. "I did everything she said. I followed her every move across that trunk."

Everyone was silent in disbelief.

"I guess it's my fault we tried to cross the tree trunk! I insisted," said Leonard. "And when Rasheed got in trouble, I

wasn't too helpful at first."

"I guess it was . . . uh, my fault for not telling Leonard I was scared of heights," said Rasheed. "I guess we weren't working together as a team."

"So you guys finally learned that cooperation is needed to survive in the wilderness. Right?" said Mr. Jones.

Leonard and Rasheed both nodded. Then Rasheed turned to Ms. Miranda.

"Thanks, Ms. Miranda. You're some pro! You saved me at that ravine!"

Leonard turned to Tiffany. "And, hey, Tiffany, you won. That's great!"

Tiffany smiled. "Maybe we can all come back here sometime. I'll show you how Juan and I made it up to the mountain top."

"It's a deal," Leonard smiled.

That evening, Ms. Miranda and Mr. Jones prepared a huge feast for the group.

They had trout, corn-on-the-cob and potatoes baked over the campfire, and a big green salad. For dessert, there were fresh wild raspberries. Mr. Jones had picked them near the trout stream.

As the group sat around the campfire later that evening, Mr. Jones called Rasheed and Leonard aside.

"Oh, no! What now?" joked Leonard.

Mr. Jones, threw his arms around their shoulders. "How would you fellows like to come back next summer as junior counselors?" he said. "I figure you two learned some important lessons about cooperation out there in the wilderness today. Maybe you could help Ms. Miranda and me teach those lessons to others! How about it?"

"Wow, that almost beats winning the tickets to the basketball game!" said Rasheed.

"Not quite. But close, very close," said Leonard, joking as usual.